GOOD NIGHT, PLANET

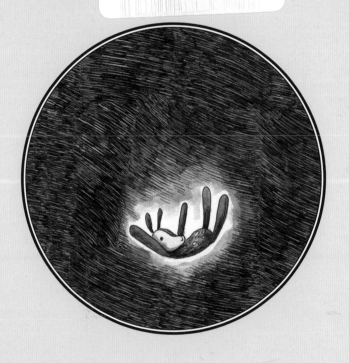

A TOON BOOK BY

LINIERS

TOON BOOKS • NEW YORK

"THIS BOOK IS FOR EMMA AND HER LOVELY PLANET." — Liniers

TOON LEVEL TWO

Editorial Director: FRANÇOISE MOULY

Book Design: FRANÇOISE MOULY & RICARDO LINIERS SIRI

RICARDO LINIERS'S artwork was done using ink and watercolor.

A TOON Book™ © 2017 Liniers & TOON Books, an imprint of RAW Junior, LLC, 27 Greene Street, New York, NY 10013. No part of this book may be used or reproduced in any manner whatsoever without written permission except in the case of brief quotations embodied in critical articles and reviews. TOON Graphics™, TOON Books®, LITTLE LIT® and TOON Into Reading!™ are trademarks of RAW Junior, LLC. All rights reserved. All our books are Smyth Sewn (the highest library-quality binding available) and printed with soy-based inks on acid-free, woodfree paper harvested from responsible sources. Printed in China by C&C Offset Printing Co., Ltd. Distributed to the trade by Consortium Book Sales and Distribution, Inc.; orders (800) 283-3572 34; orderentry@perseusbooks.com; www.cbsd.com. Library of Congress Cataloging-in-Publication Data available at https://lccn.loc.gov/2017013136. A Spanish edition, *Buenas Noches, Planeta*, is also available.

ISBN 978-1-943145-20-1 (hardcover English edition)
ISBN 978-1-943145-21-8 (hardcover Spanish edition)
ISBN 978-1-943145-19-5 (softcover Spanish edition)
17 18 19 20 21 22 C&C 10 9 8 7 6 5 4 3 2 1

FOR FREE CCSS-ALIGNED LESSON PLANS & ACTIVITY SHEETS, VISIT
WWW.TOON-BOOKS.COM

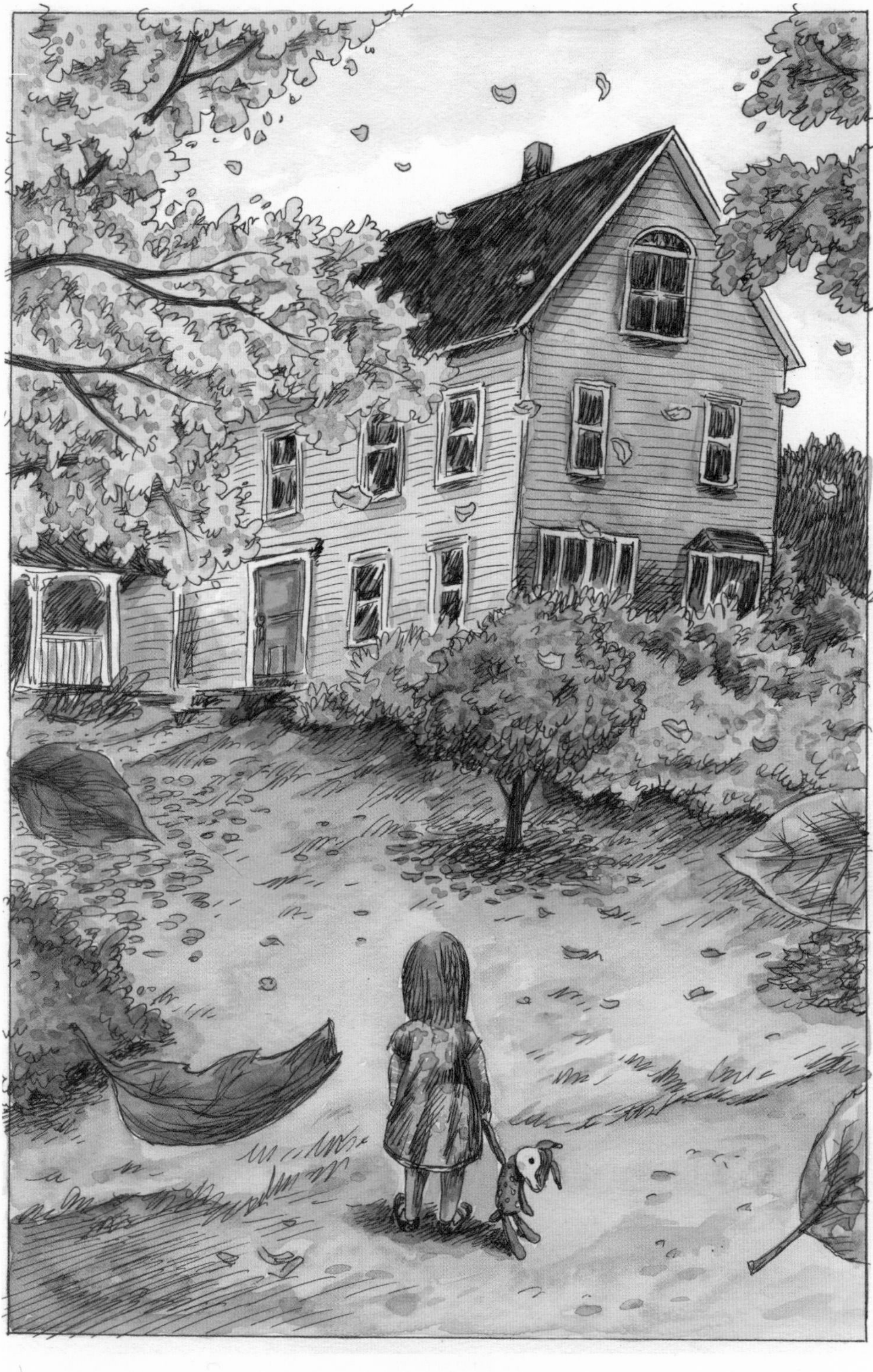

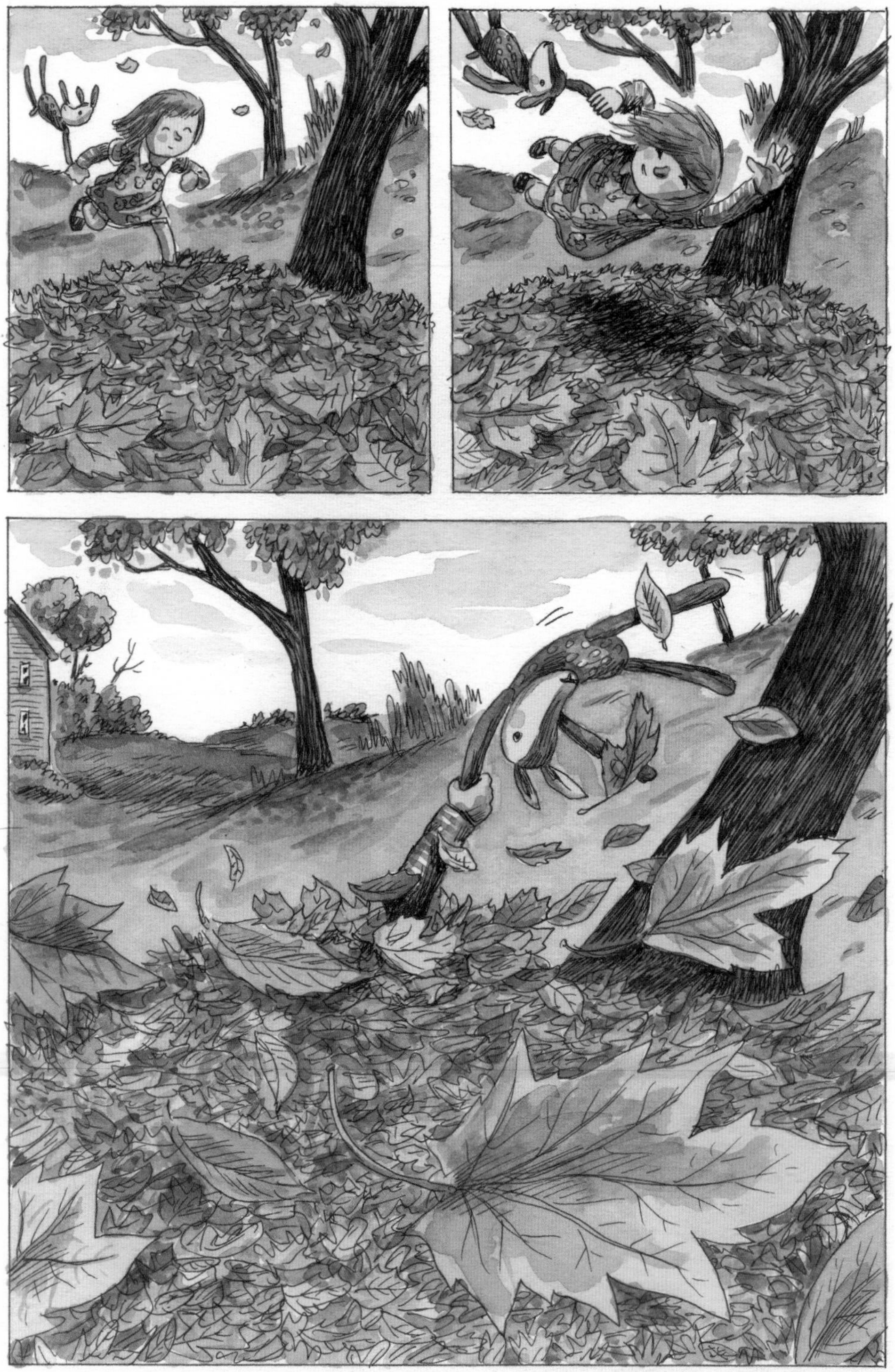

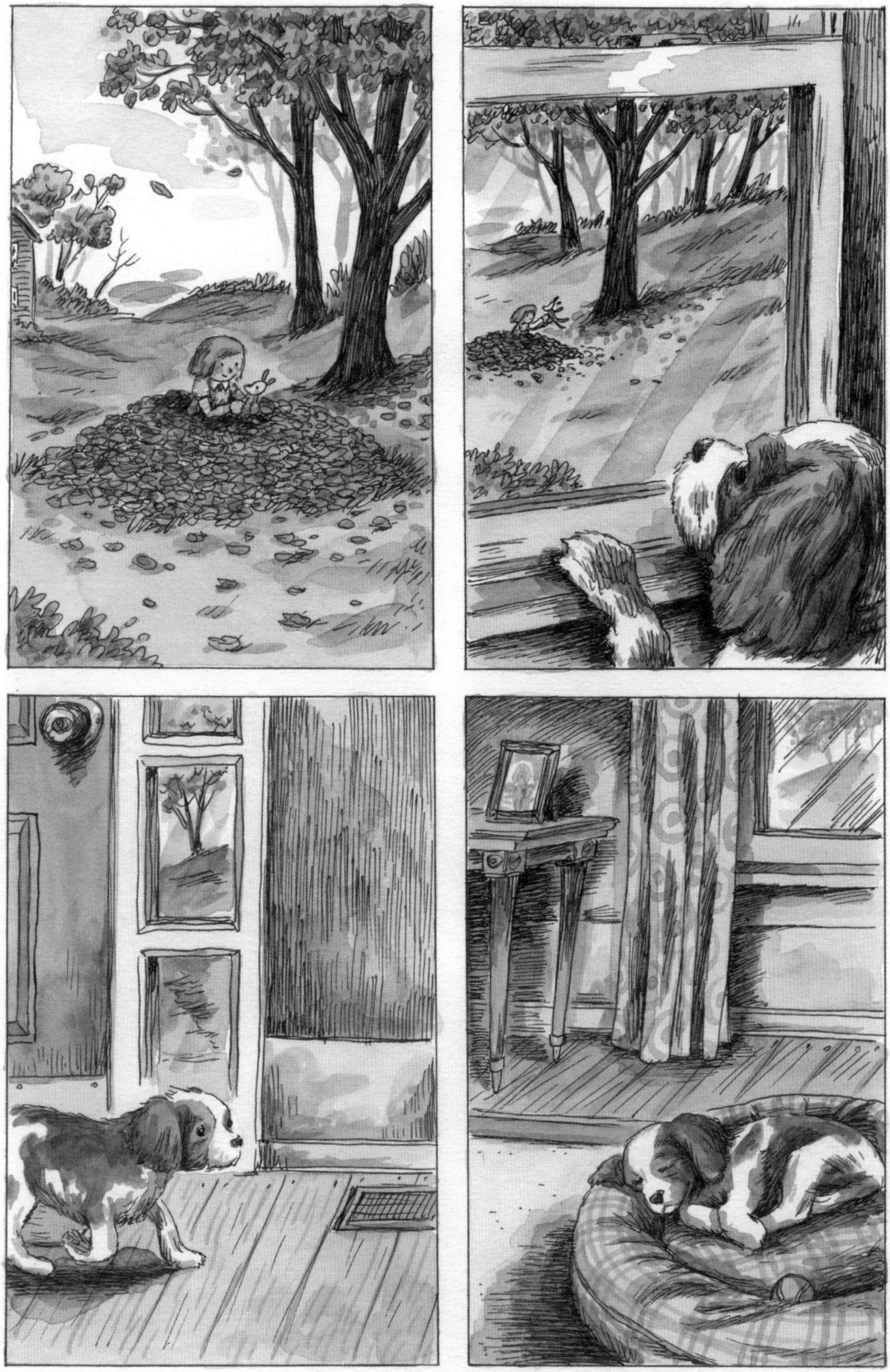

HAT

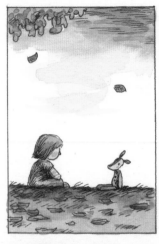

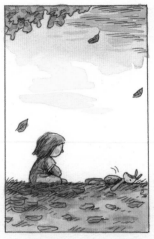

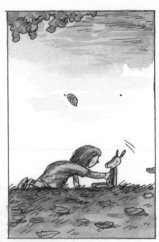

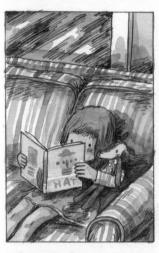

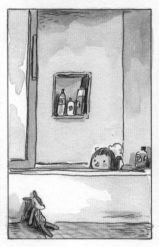

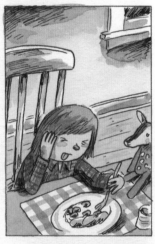

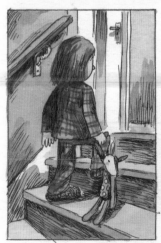

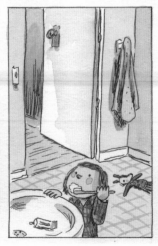

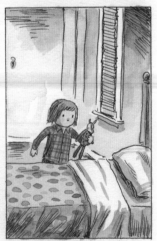

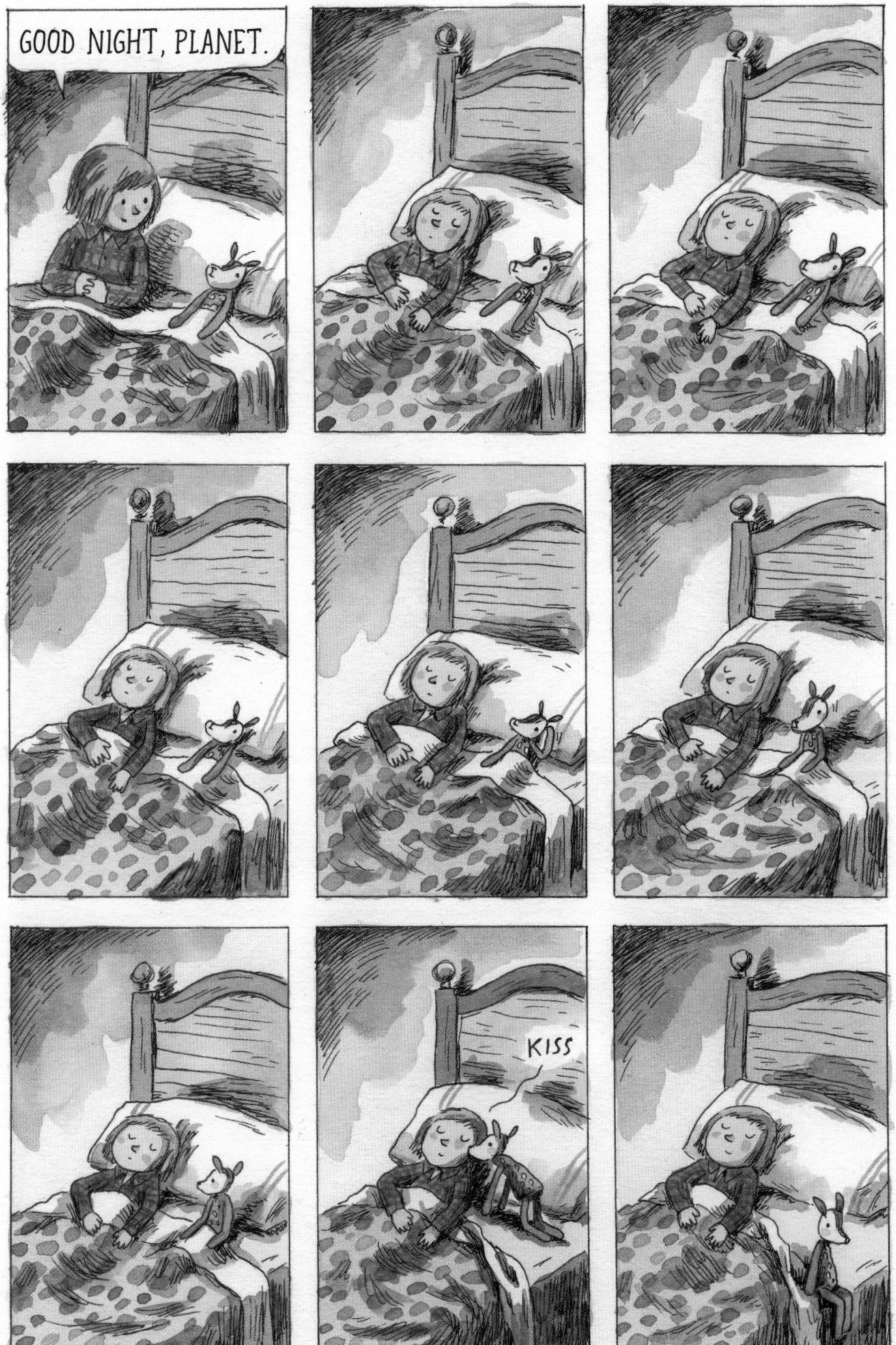
GOOD NIGHT, PLANET.
KISS

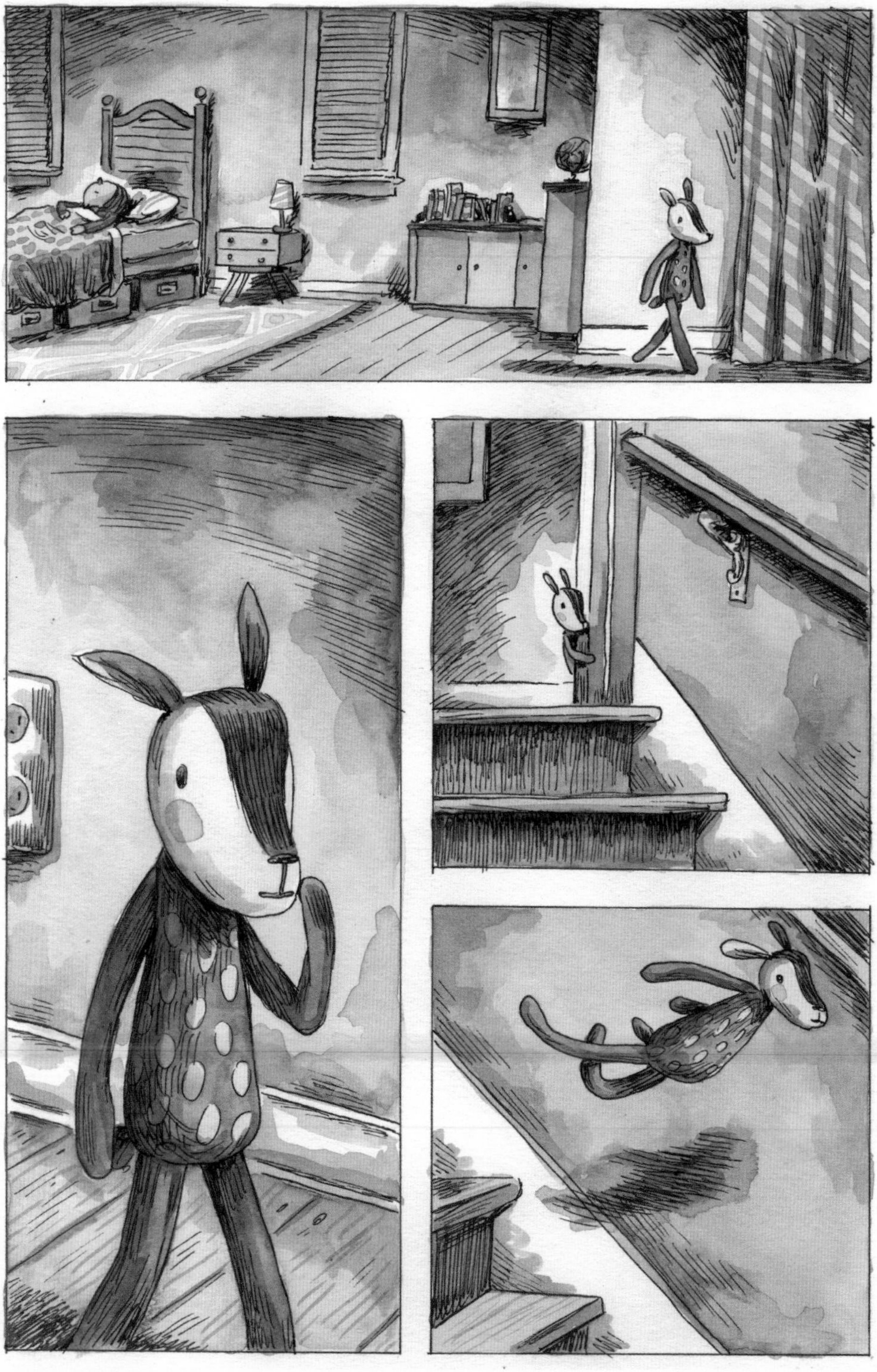

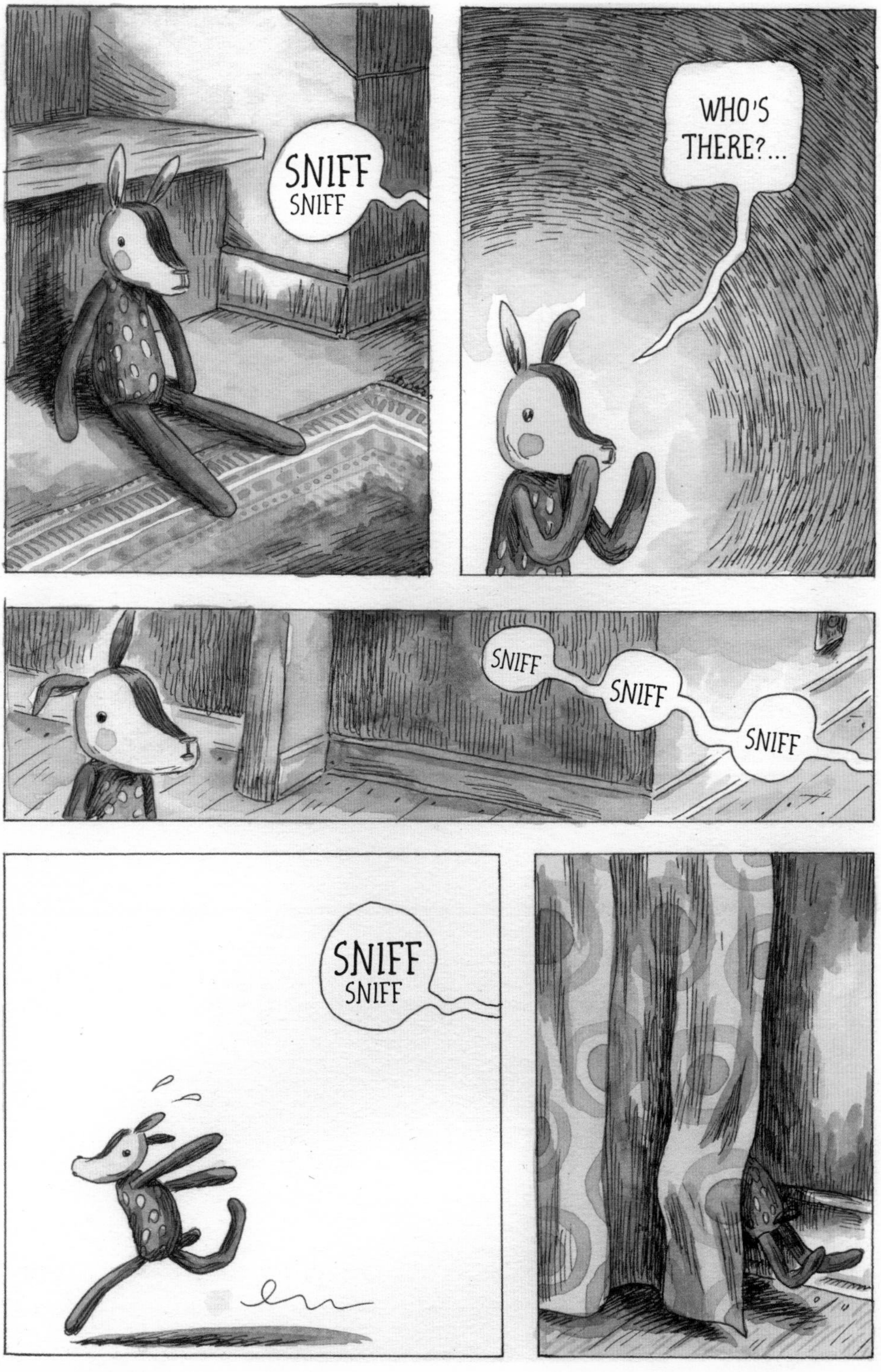
SNIFF SNIFF
WHO'S THERE?...
SNIFF
SNIFF
SNIFF
SNIFF SNIFF

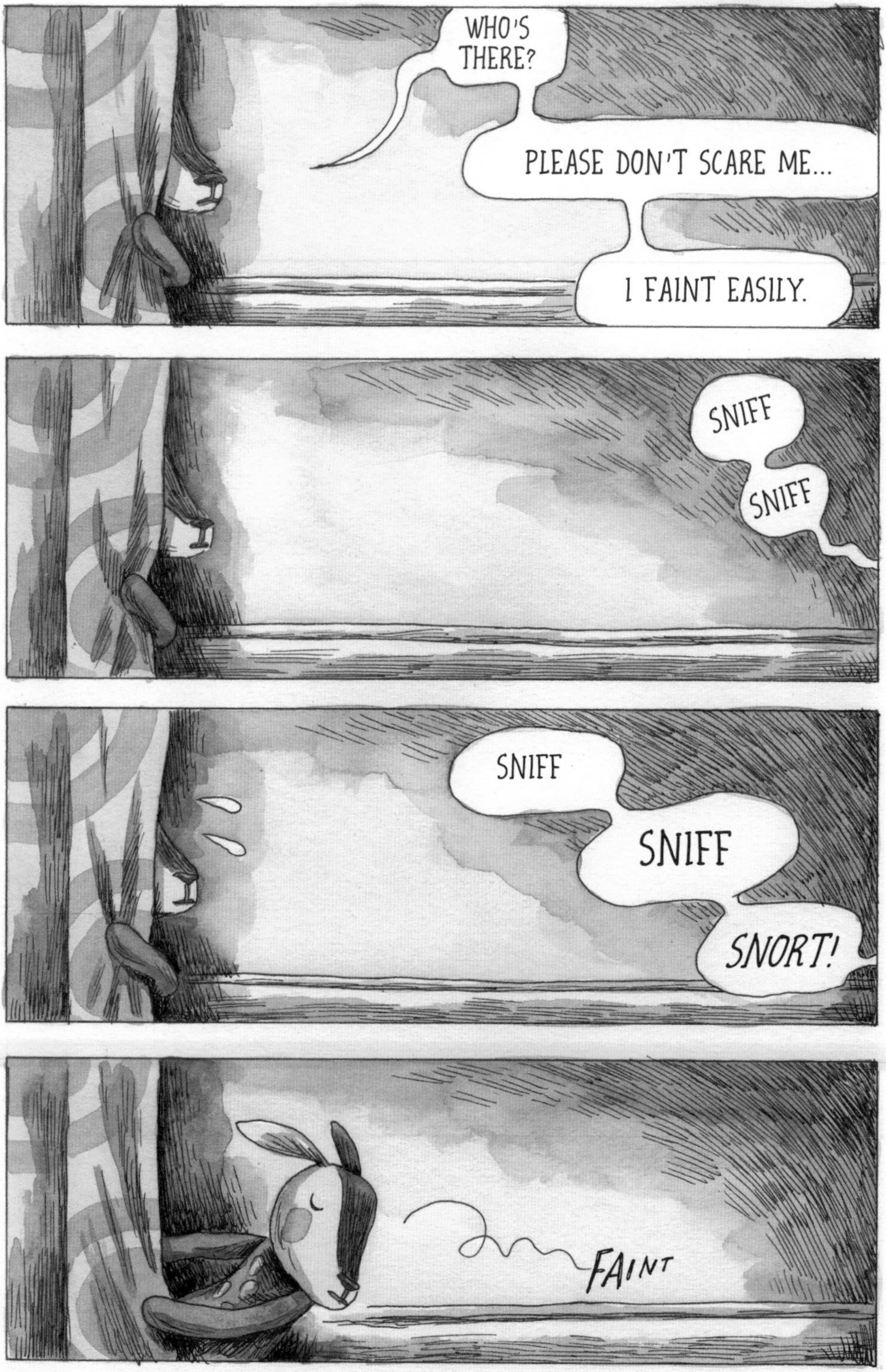
WHO'S THERE?
PLEASE DON'T SCARE ME...
I FAINT EASILY.
SNIFF
SNIFF
SNIFF
SNIFF
SNORT!
FAINT

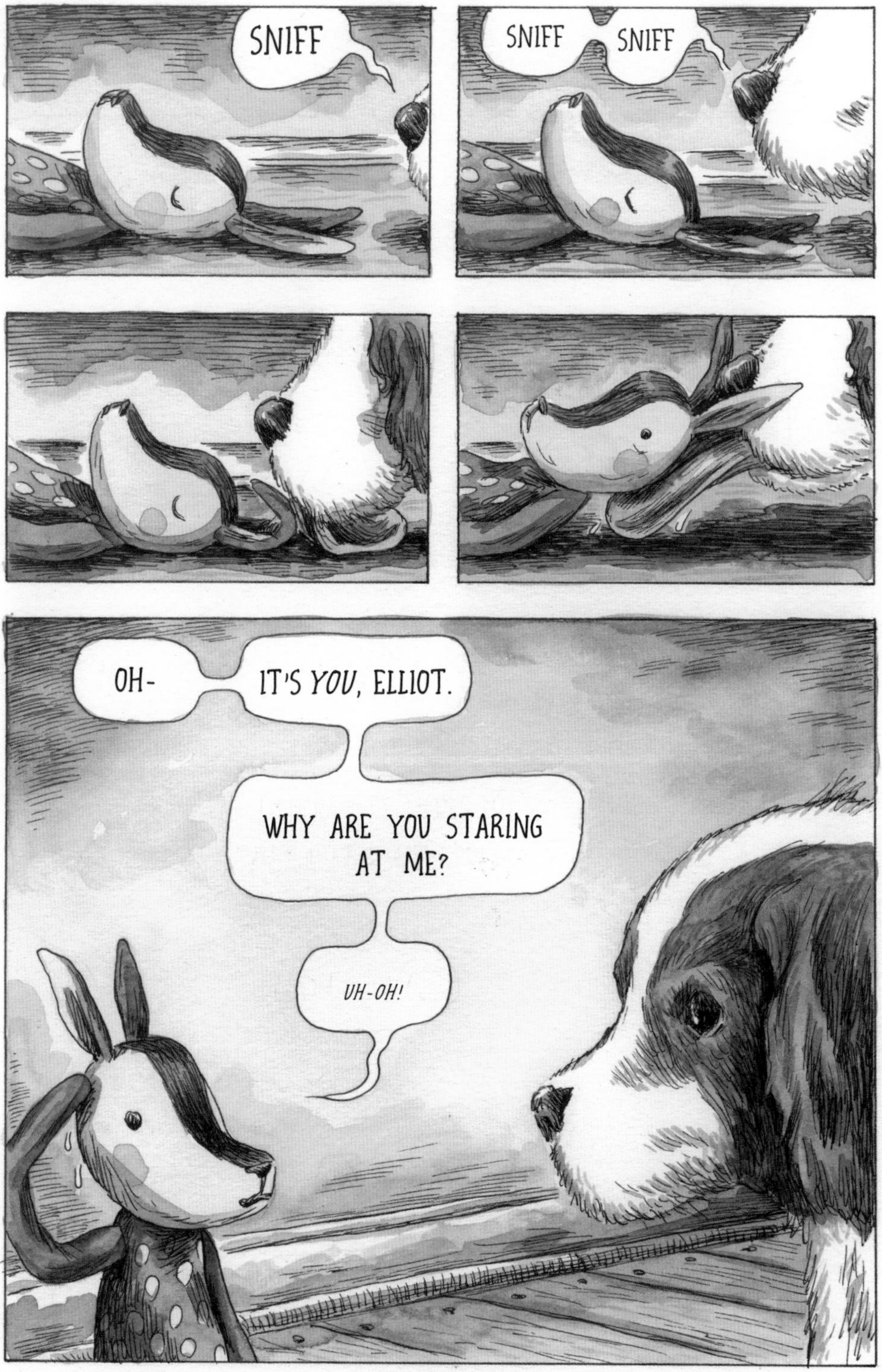
SNIFF
SNIFF SNIFF
OH- IT'S *YOU*, ELLIOT.
WHY ARE YOU STARING AT ME?
UH-OH!

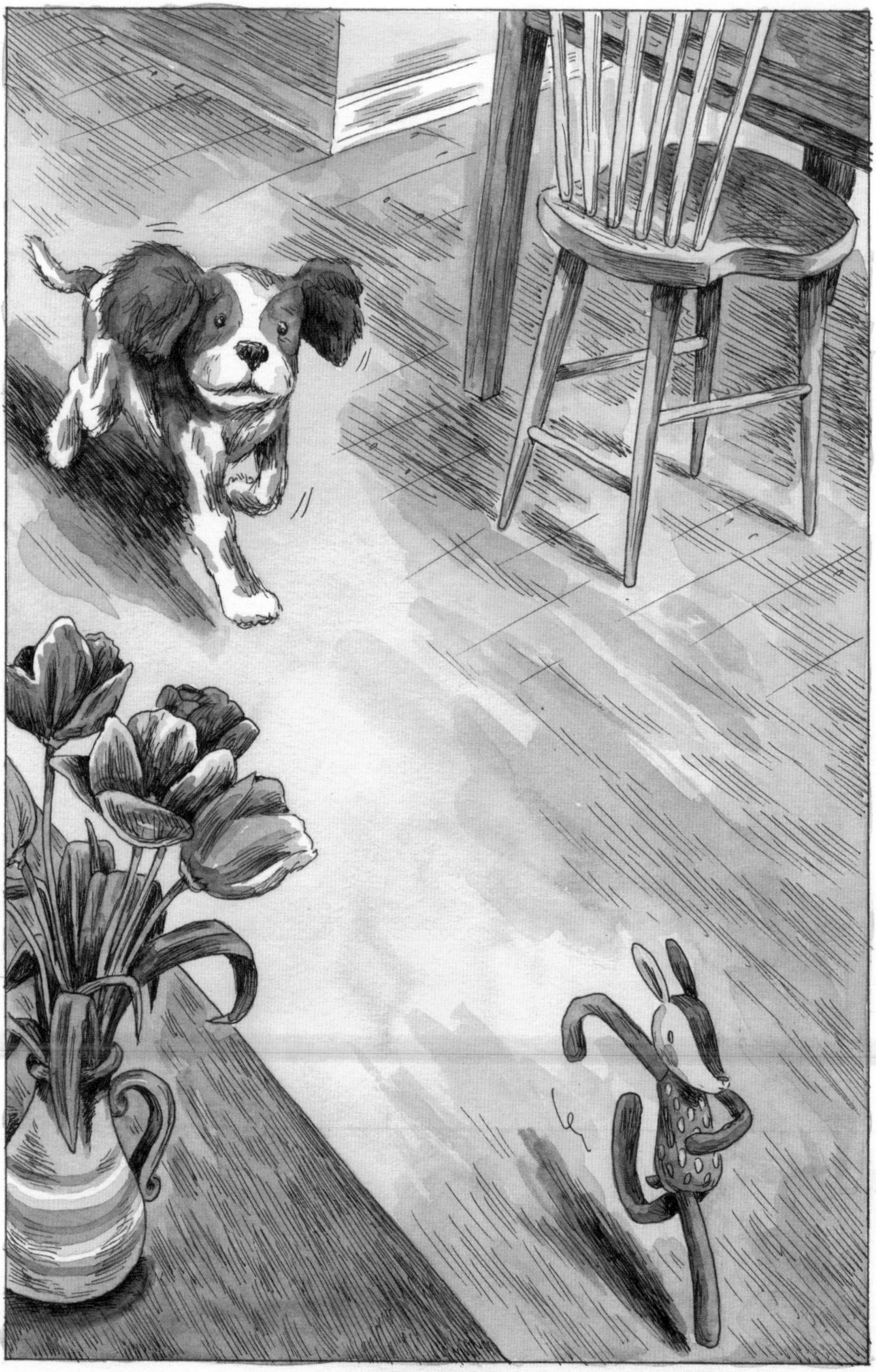

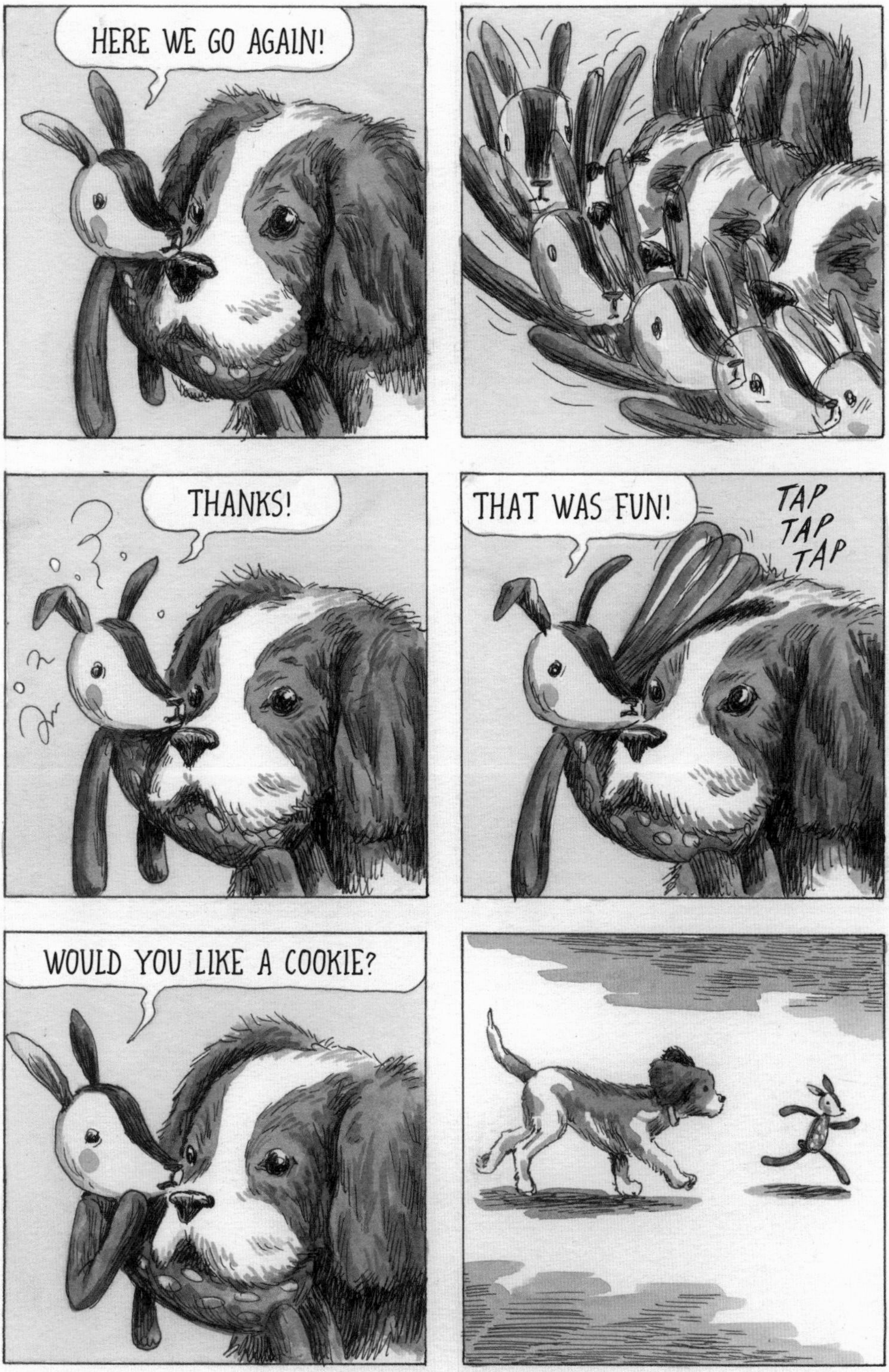
HERE WE GO AGAIN!
THANKS!
THAT WAS FUN!
TAP TAP TAP
WOULD YOU LIKE A COOKIE?

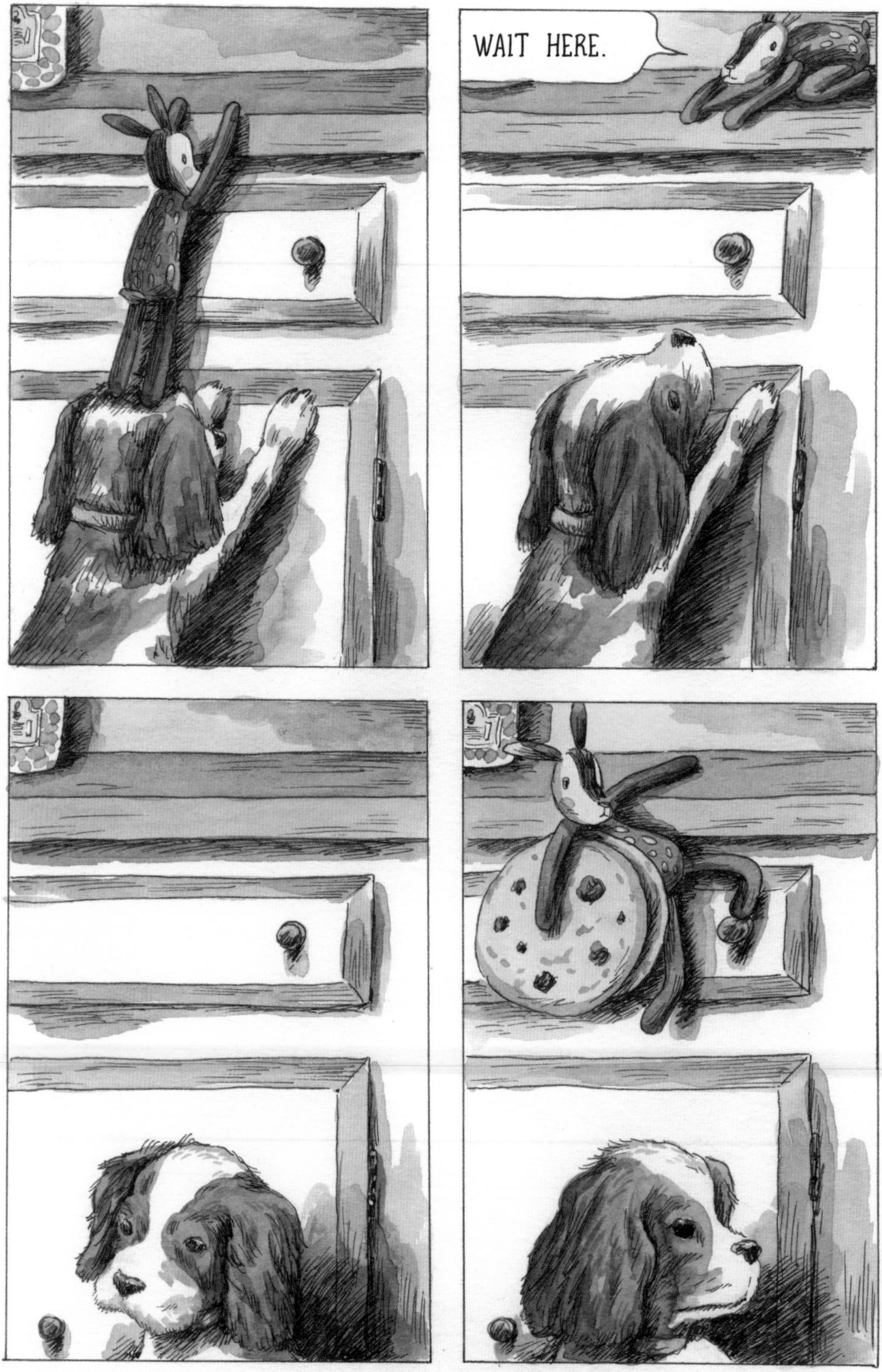
WAIT HERE.

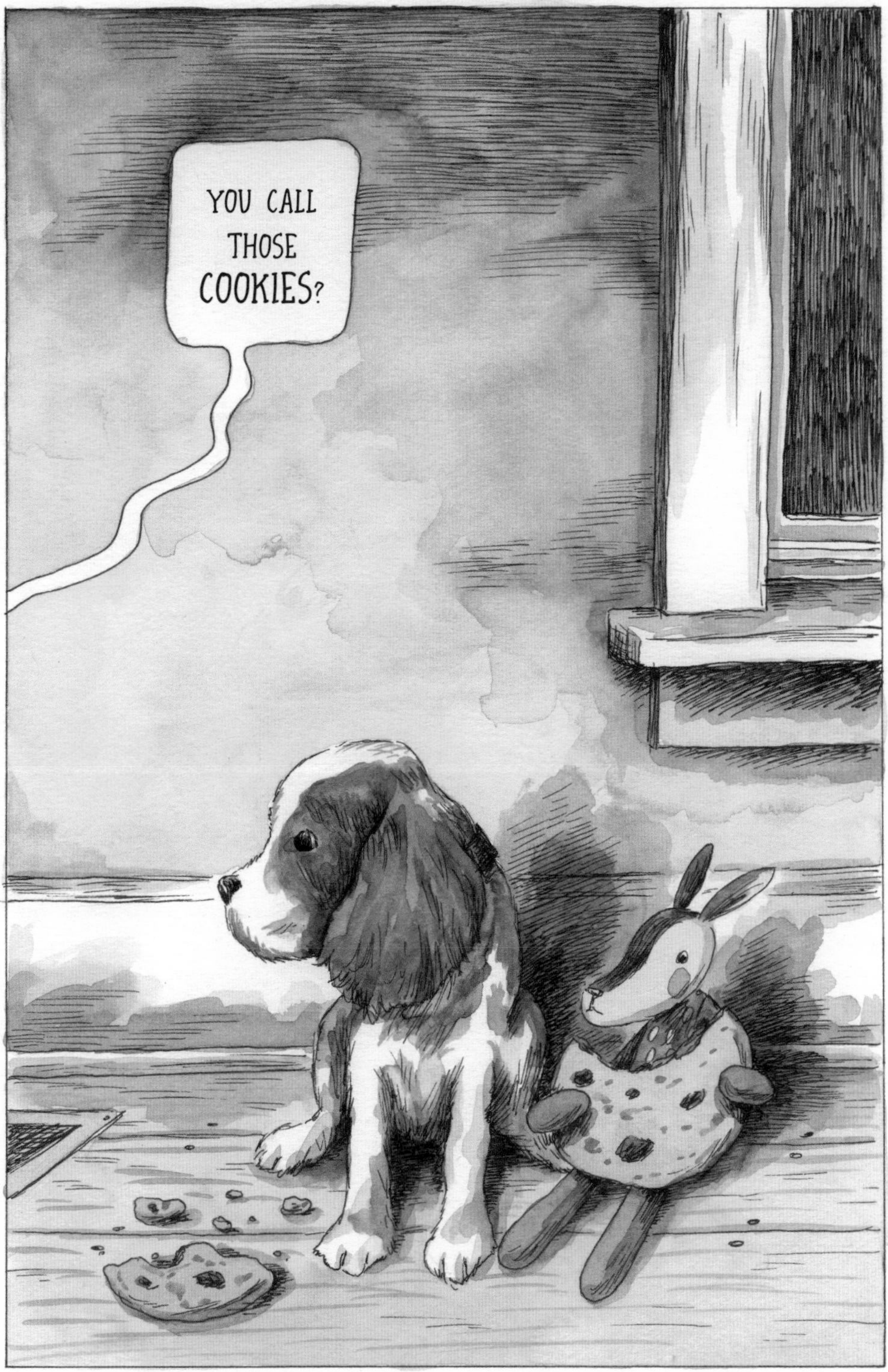
YOU CALL THOSE COOKIES?

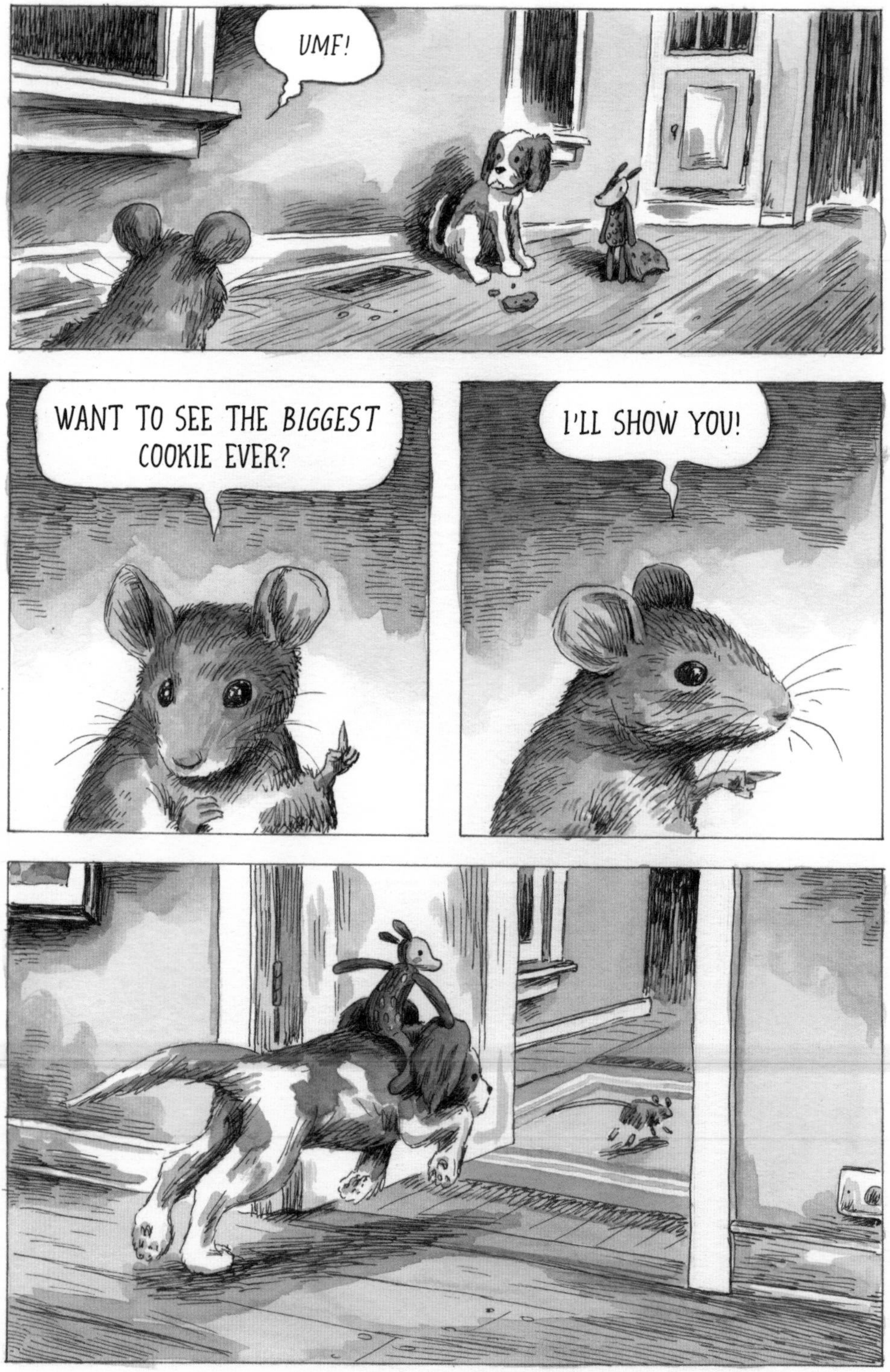
UMF!
WANT TO SEE THE *BIGGEST* COOKIE EVER?
I'LL SHOW YOU!

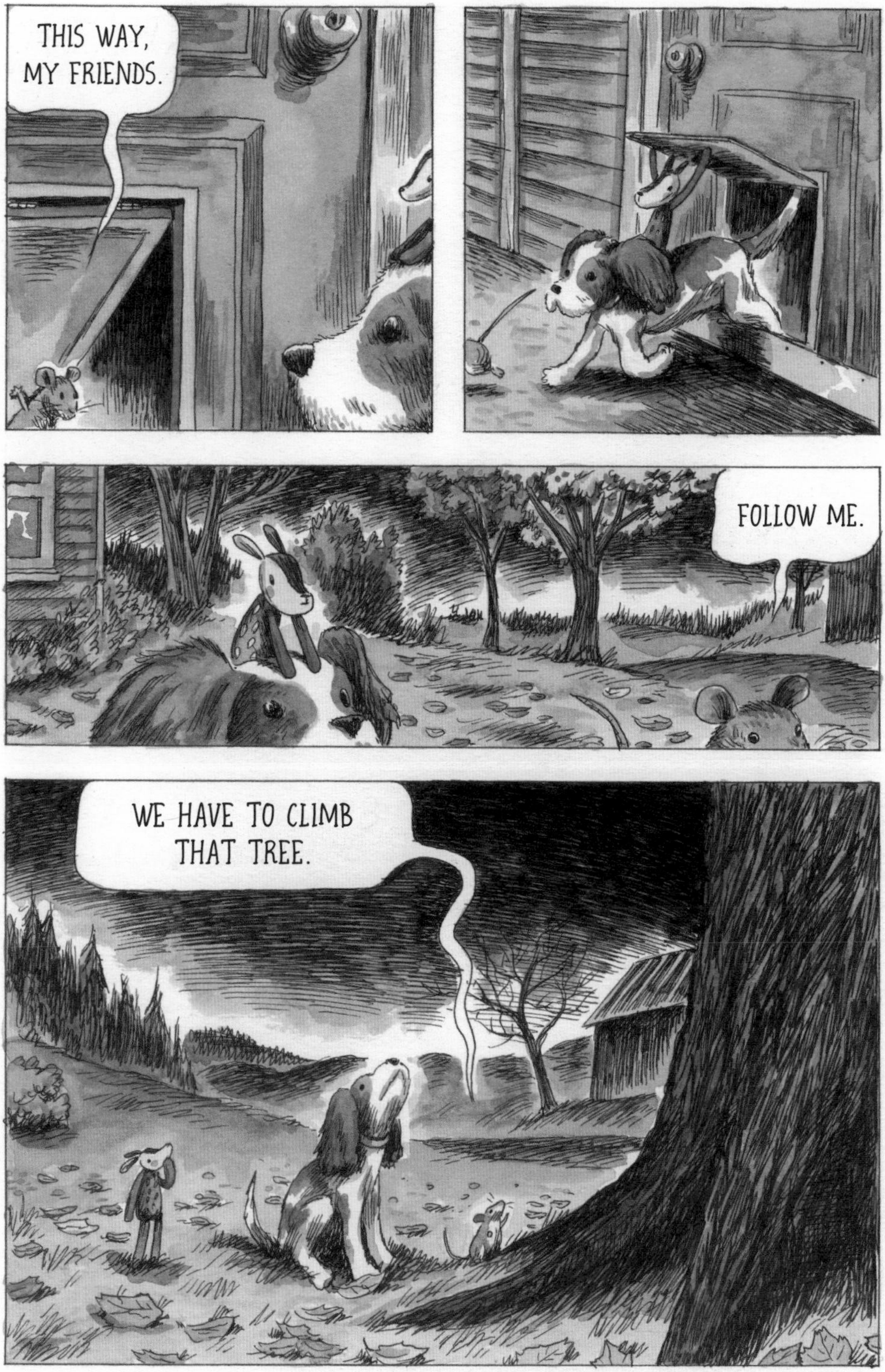
THIS WAY, MY FRIENDS.
FOLLOW ME.
WE HAVE TO CLIMB THAT TREE.

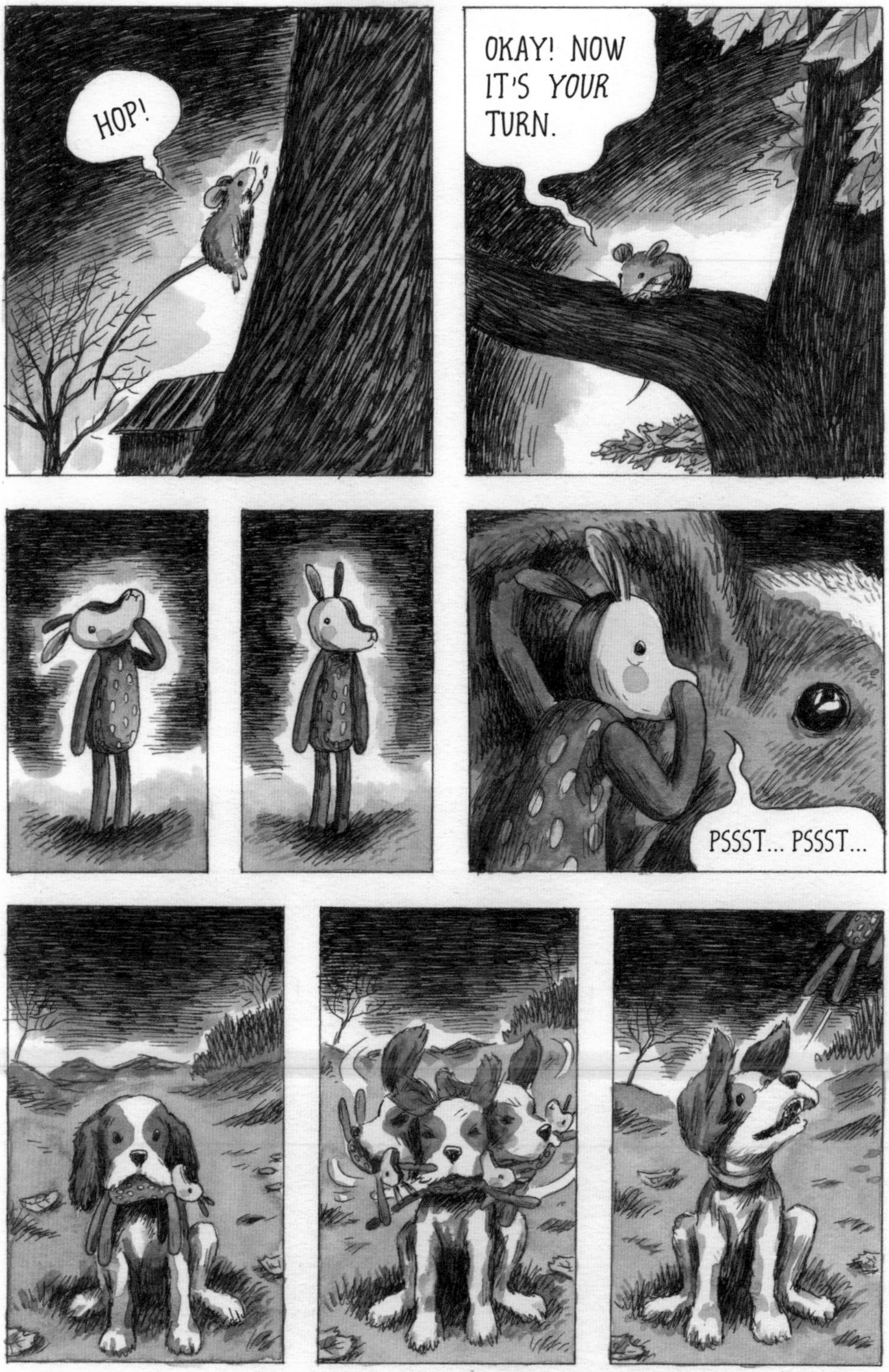
HOP!
OKAY! NOW IT'S *YOUR* TURN.
PSSST... PSSST...

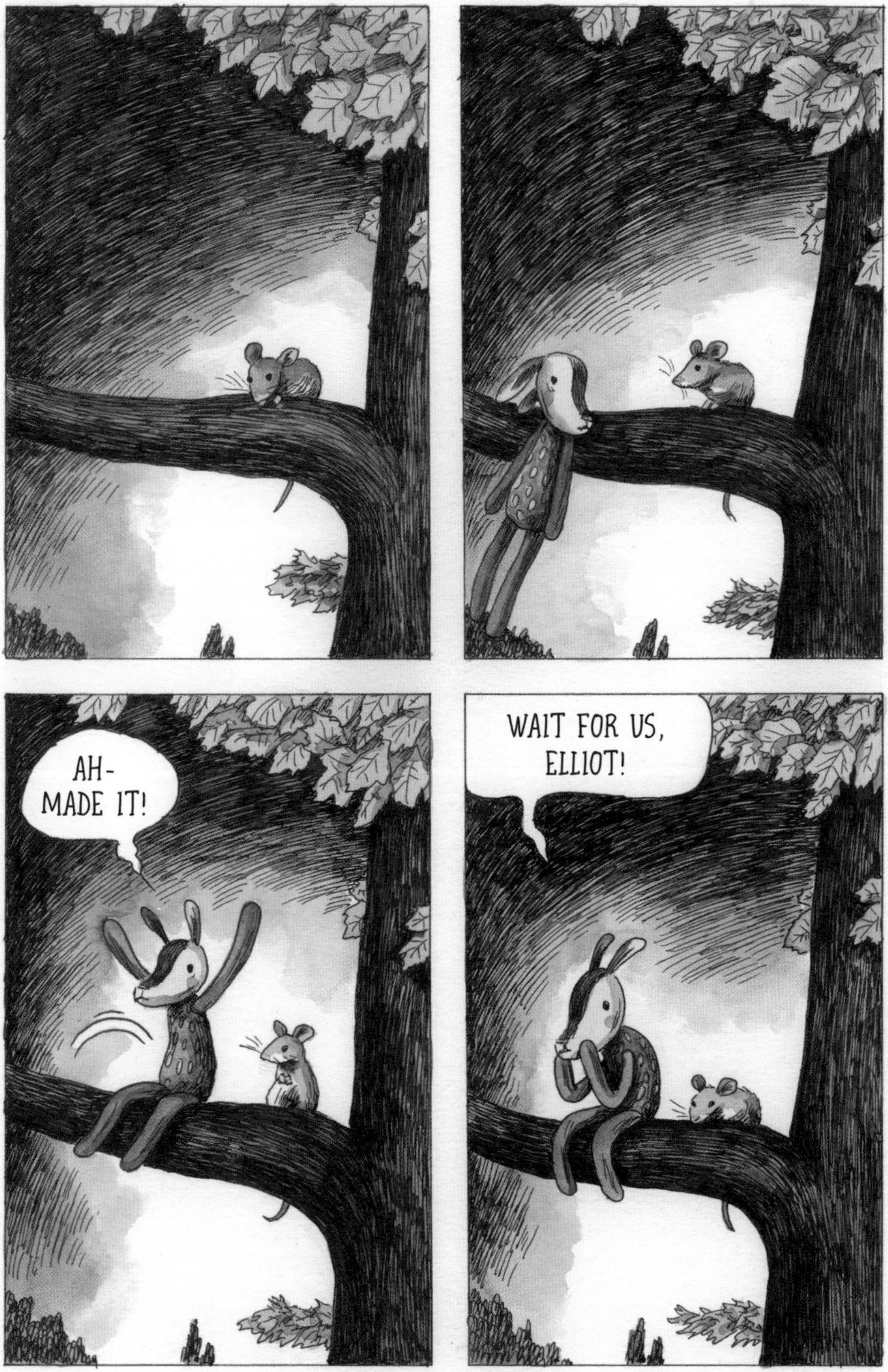
AH-
MADE IT!
WAIT FOR US,
ELLIOT!

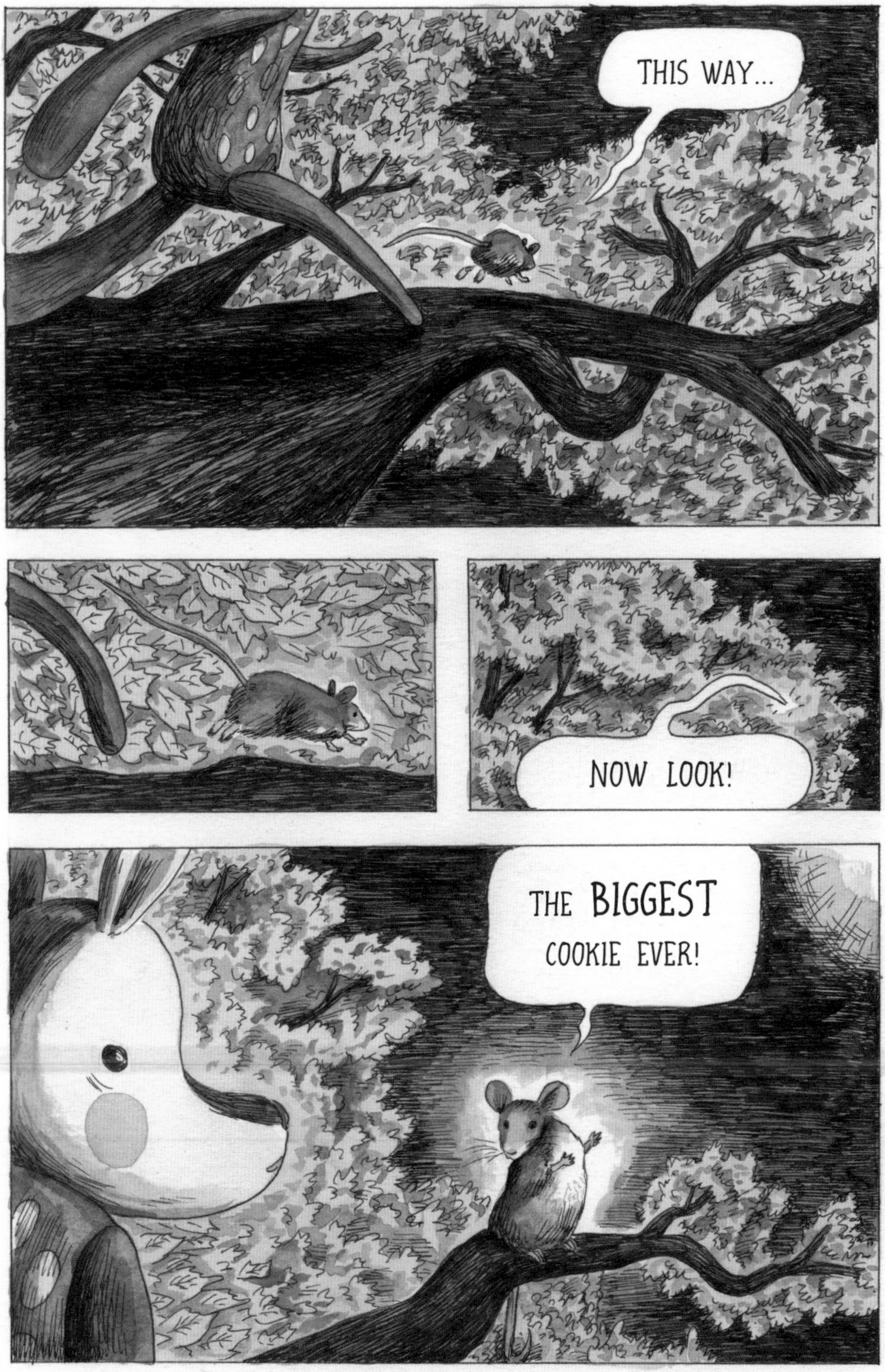
THIS WAY...
NOW LOOK!
THE BIGGEST COOKIE EVER!

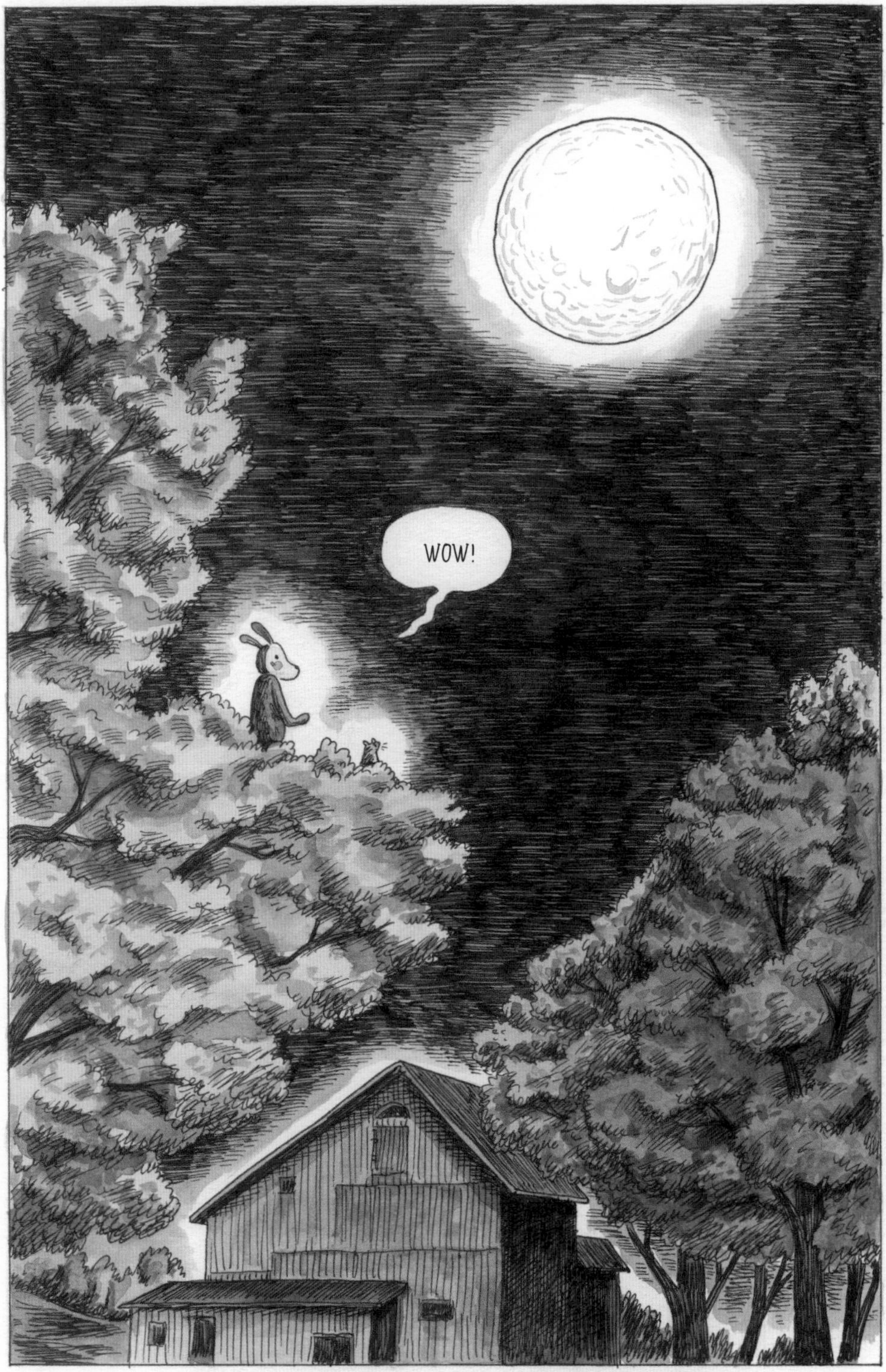
WOW!

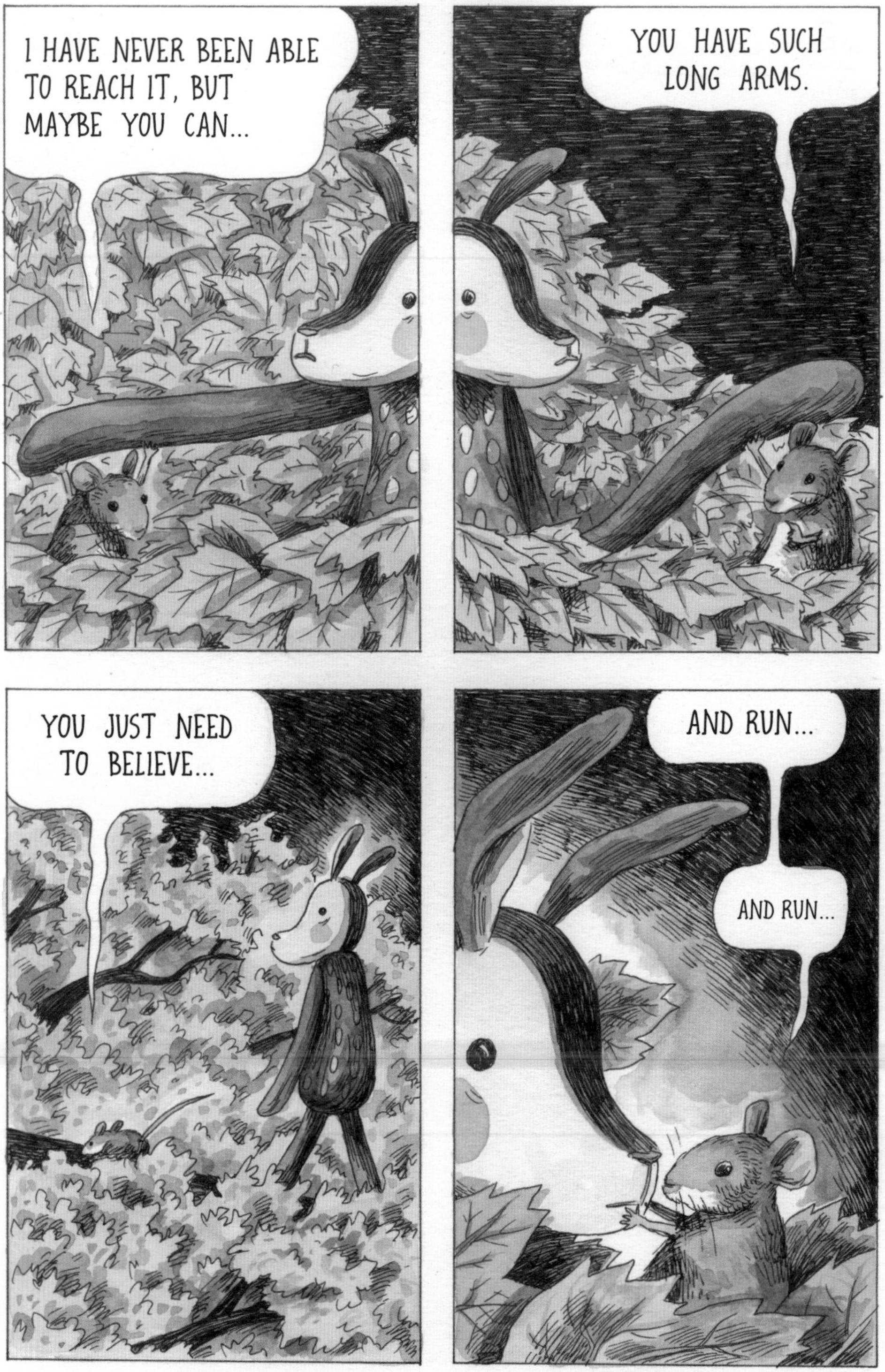
I HAVE NEVER BEEN ABLE TO REACH IT, BUT MAYBE YOU CAN...
YOU HAVE SUCH LONG ARMS.
YOU JUST NEED TO BELIEVE...
AND RUN...
AND RUN...

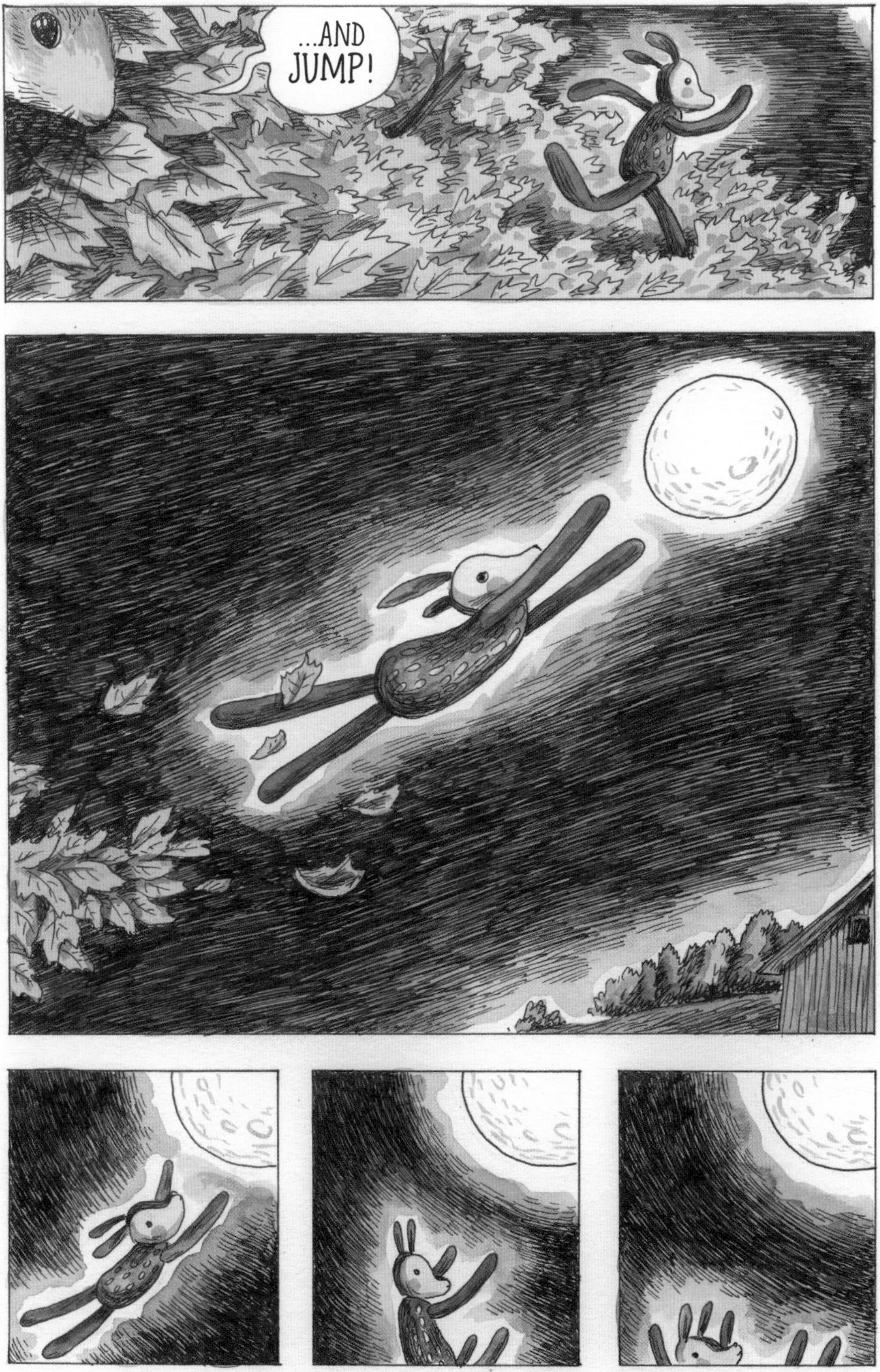
...AND JUMP!

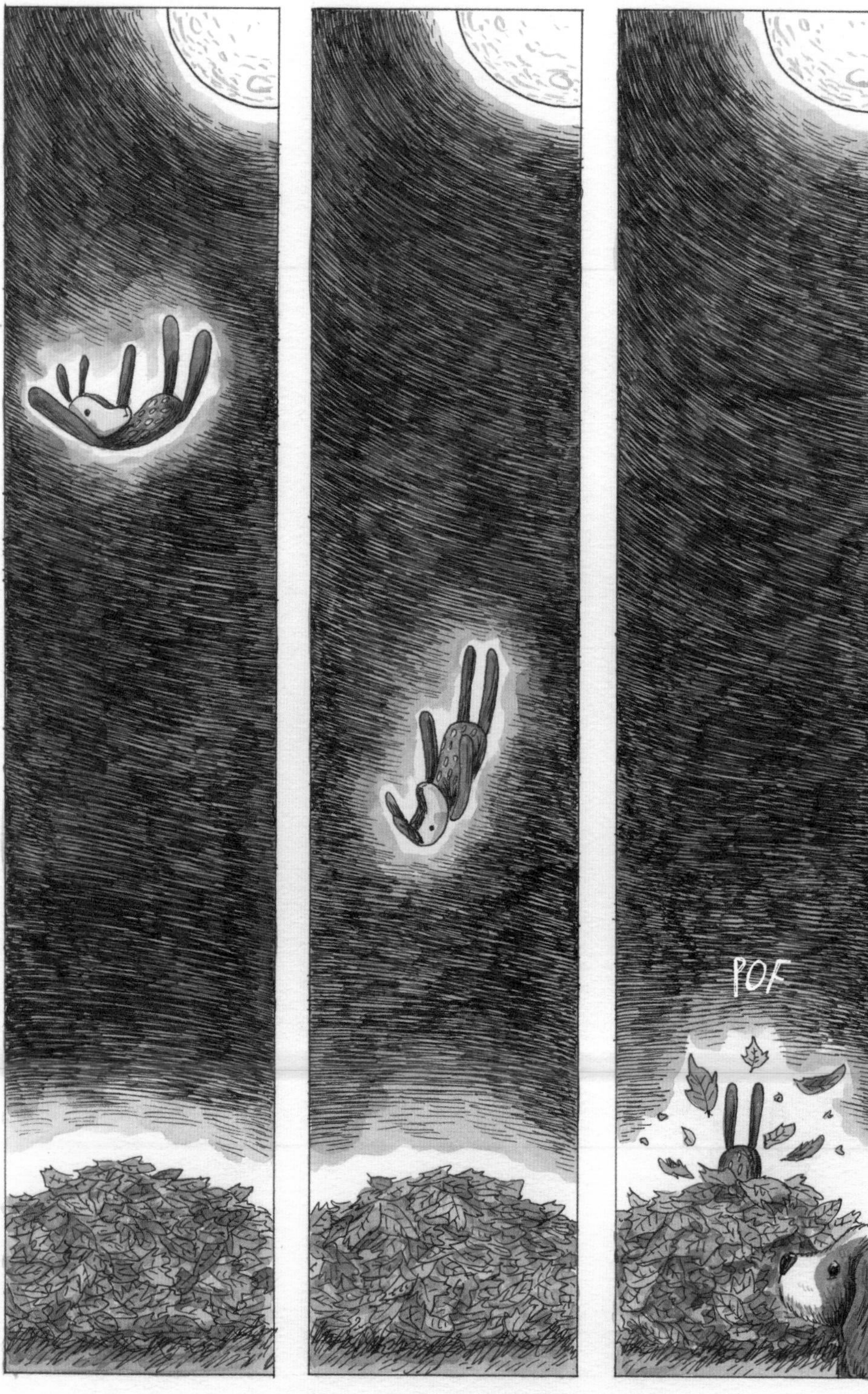
POF

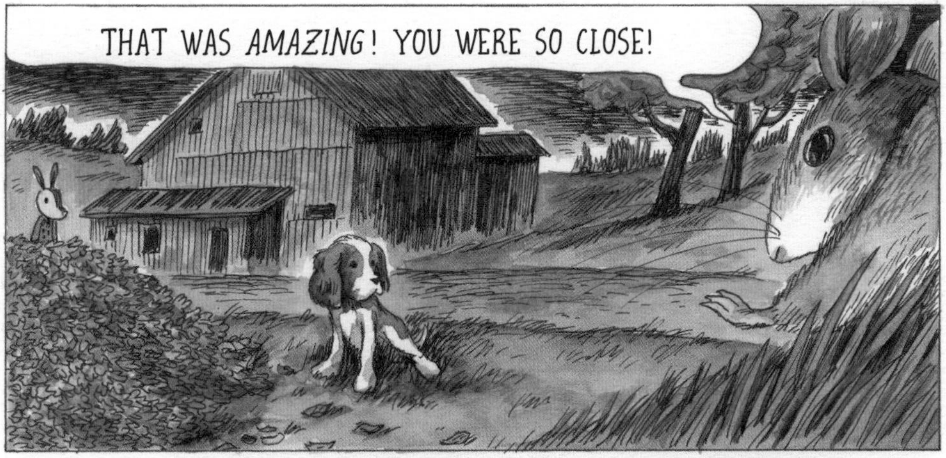
THAT WAS *AMAZING*! YOU WERE SO CLOSE!

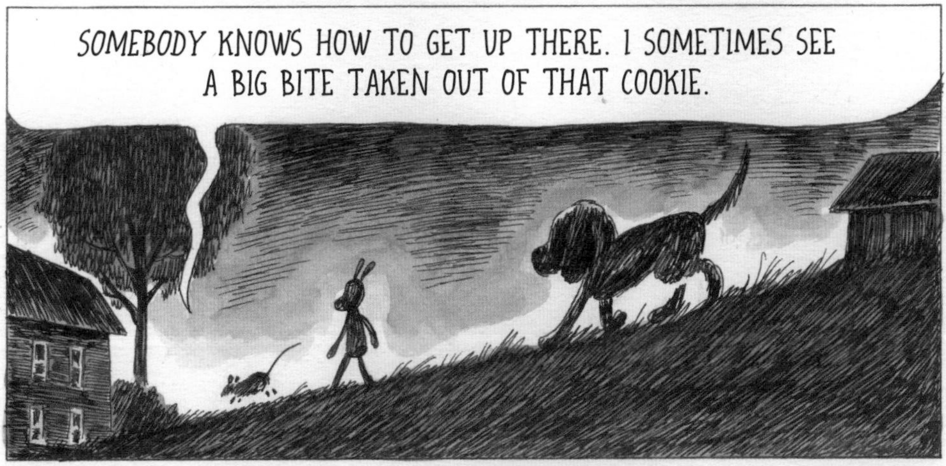
SOMEBODY KNOWS HOW TO GET UP THERE. I SOMETIMES SEE A BIG BITE TAKEN OUT OF THAT COOKIE.

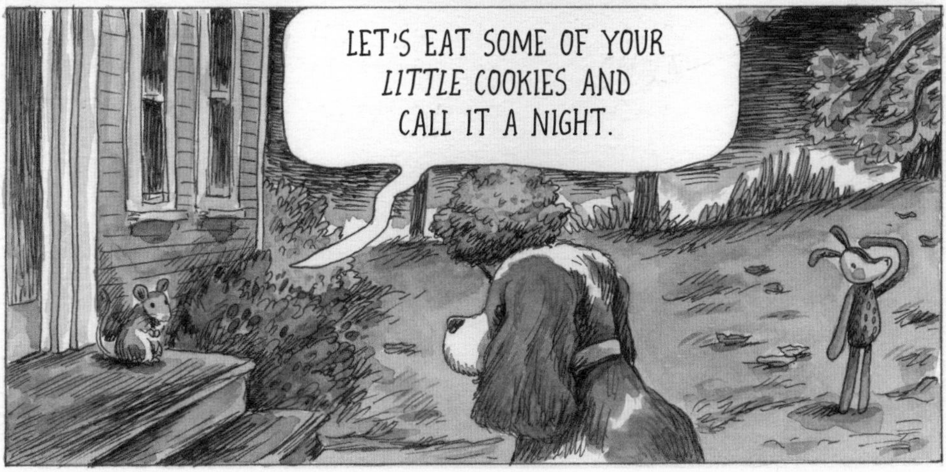
LET'S EAT SOME OF YOUR *LITTLE* COOKIES AND CALL IT A NIGHT.

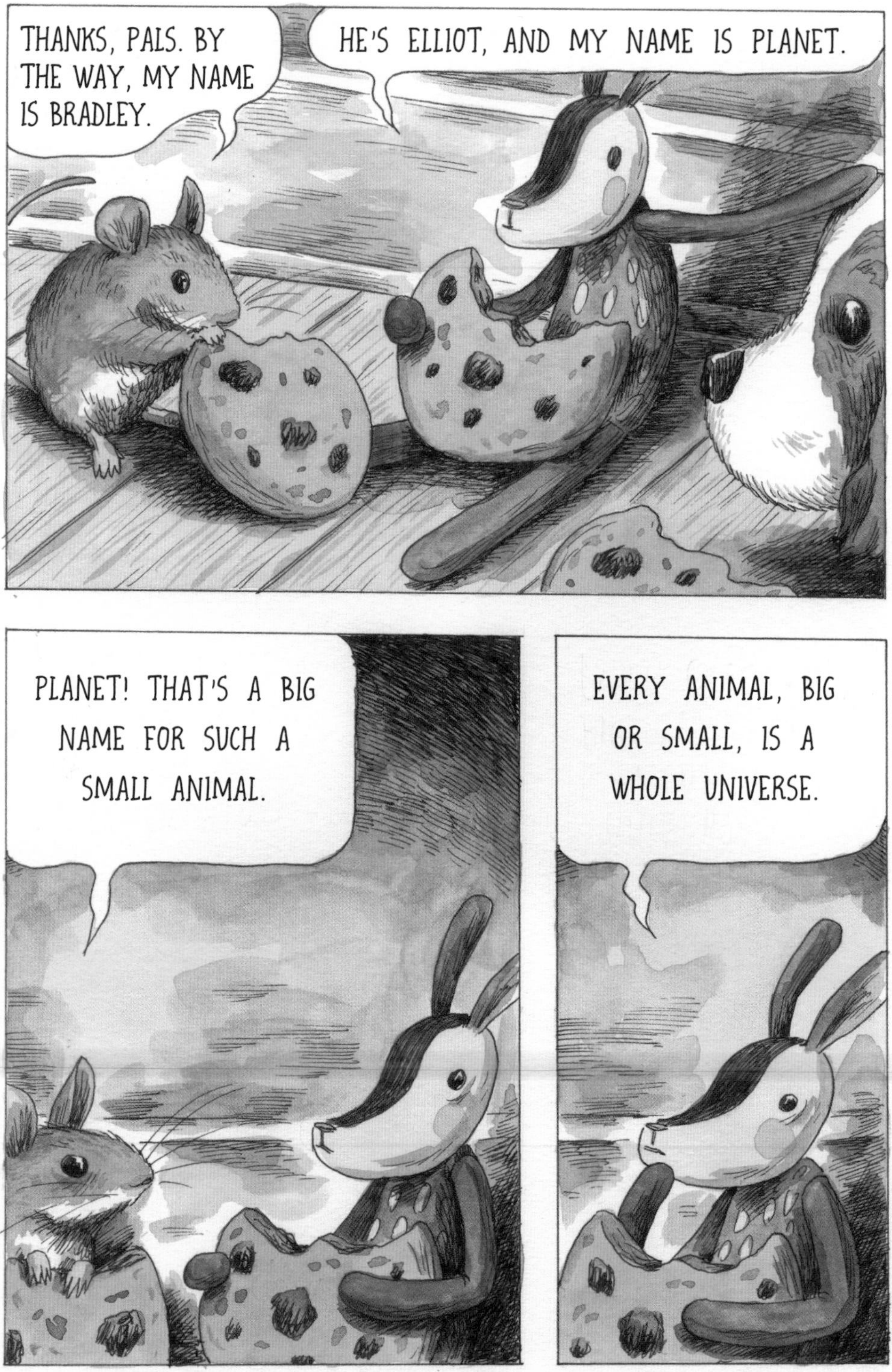
THANKS, PALS. BY THE WAY, MY NAME IS BRADLEY.
HE'S ELLIOT, AND MY NAME IS PLANET.
PLANET! THAT'S A BIG NAME FOR SUCH A SMALL ANIMAL.
EVERY ANIMAL, BIG OR SMALL, IS A WHOLE UNIVERSE.

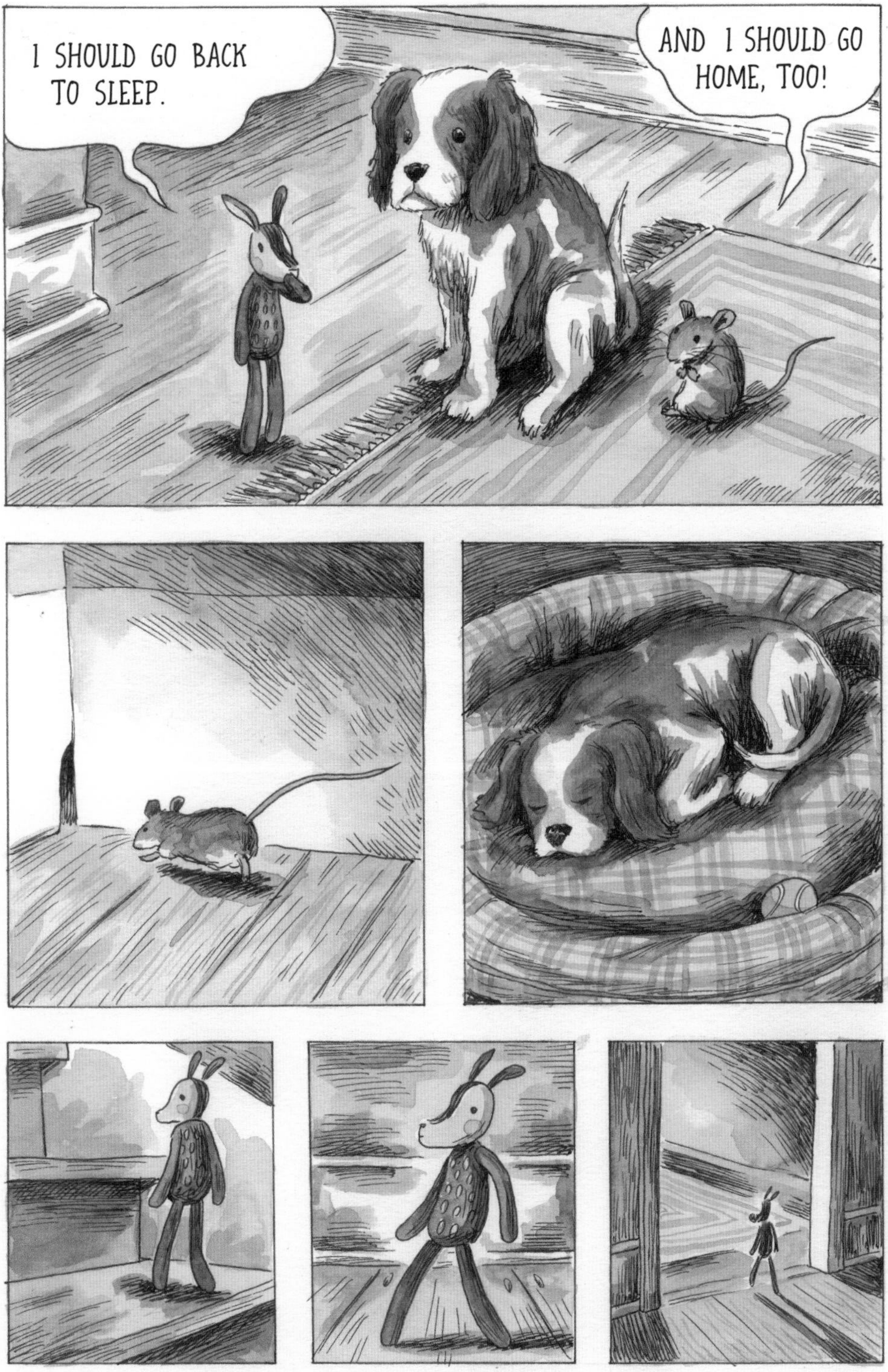
I SHOULD GO BACK TO SLEEP.
AND I SHOULD GO HOME, TOO!

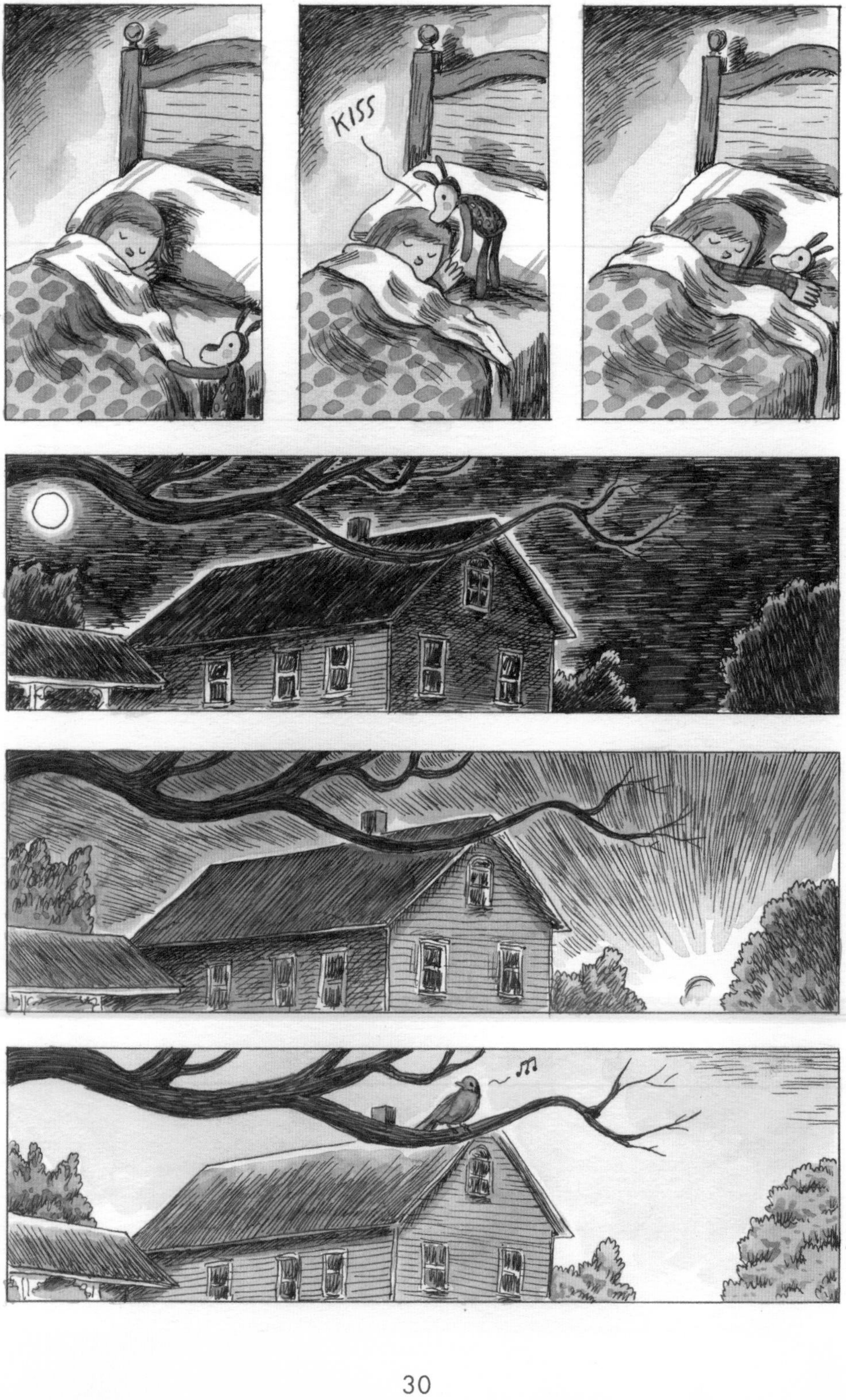
KISS

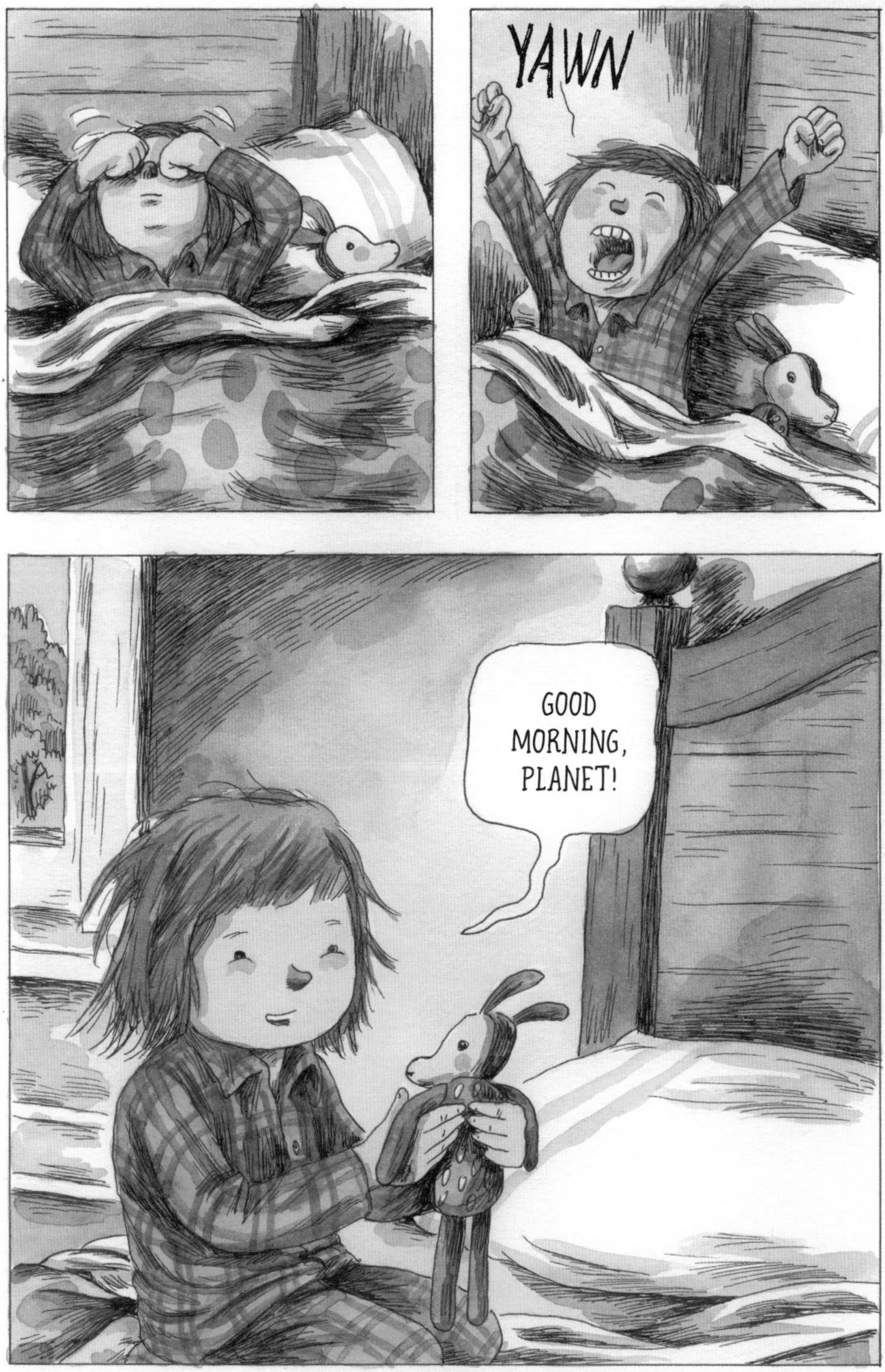
YAWN
GOOD MORNING, PLANET!

THE END

ABOUT THE AUTHOR

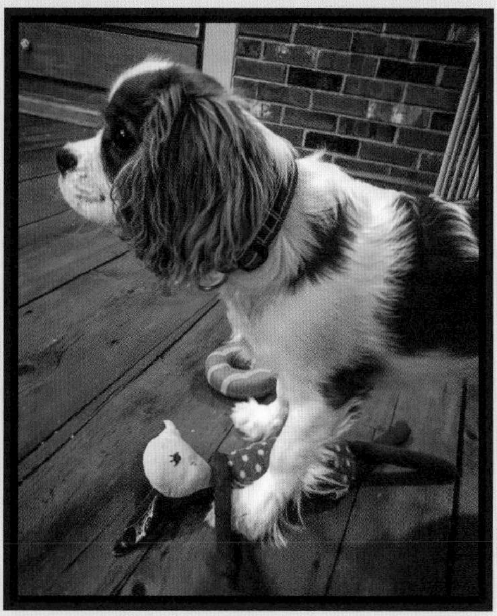

LINIERS's U.S. debut, the TOON Book *The Big Wet Balloon*, was nominated for an Eisner Award and selected as one of *Parents Magazine*'s Top 10. His TOON follow-up, *Written and Drawn by Henrietta*, was named one of *School Library Journal*'s Best Books of the Year. Ricardo Liniers Siri is from Buenos Aires, Argentina, but he now lives in Vermont as the artist-in-residence at the Center for Cartoon Studies. He, his wife, their three daughters, and their puppy Elliot (above, with Planet) love looking at the night sky in New England. He was inspired to write this book after he got his youngest daughter, Emma, a new stuffed animal. Ricardo says, "Emma was just two and a half at the time. I asked her, 'What's the name of your new dolly?' and she blurted out one of the words she had recently learned: 'Planet!' It was the absolutely perfect name."

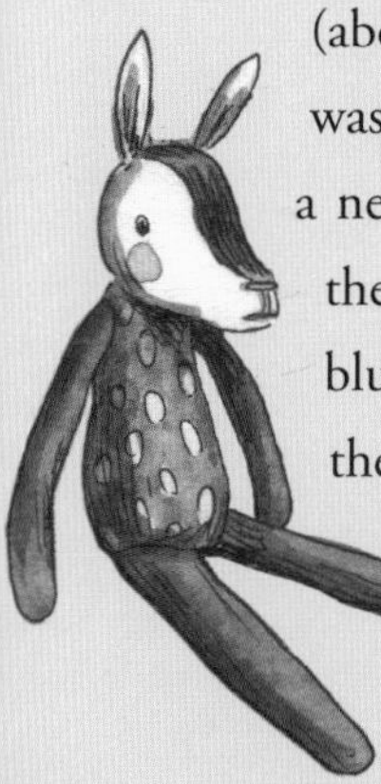

TIPS FOR PARENTS AND TEACHERS:
HOW TO READ COMICS WITH KIDS

Kids **love** comics! They are naturally drawn to the details in the pictures, which make them want to read the words. Comics beg for repeated readings and let both emerging and reluctant readers enjoy complex stories with a rich vocabulary. But since comics have their own grammar, here are a few tips for reading them with kids:

GUIDE YOUNG READERS: Use your finger to show your place in the text, but keep it at the bottom of the speaking character so it doesn't hide the very important facial expressions.

HAM IT UP! Think of the comic book story as a play, and don't hesitate to read with expression and intonation. Assign parts or get kids to supply the sound effects, a great way to reinforce phonics skills.

LET THEM GUESS. Comics provide lots of context for the words so emerging readers can make informed guesses. Like jigsaw puzzles, comics ask readers to make connections, so check a young audience's understanding by asking, "What's this character thinking?" (But don't be surprised if a kid finds some of the comics' subtle details faster than you).

TALK ABOUT THE PICTURES. Point out how the artist paces the story with pauses (silent panels) or speeded-up action (a burst of short panels). Discuss how the size and shape of the panels carry meaning.

ABOVE ALL, ENJOY! There is of course never one right way to read, so go for the shared pleasure. Once children make the story happen in their imagination, they have discovered the thrill of reading, and you won't be able to stop them. At that point, just go get them more books, and more comics.

www.TOON-BOOKS.com
SEE OUR FREE ONLINE CARTOON MAKERS, LESSON PLANS, AND MUCH MORE.